MYTH·MEN™

GUARDIANS OF THE LEGEND

ATALANTA

THE WILD GIRL

BY LAURA GERINGER

ILLUSTRATED BY PETER BOLLINGER

SCHOLASTIC INC.

NEW YORK TORONTO LONDON AUCKLAND SYDNEY

For my mother with love. —L. G.   *For my family.* —P. B.

No part of this publication may be reproduced in whole or in part, or stored in a retrieval system, or transmitted in any form or by any means, electronic, mechanical, photocopying, recording, or otherwise, without written permission of the publisher. For information regarding permission, write to Scholastic Inc., 555 Broadway, New York, NY 10012. • ISBN 0-590-84552-7

Text copyright © 1997 by Laura Geringer. • Illustrations copyright © 1997 by Peter Bollinger. MYTH MEN is a trademark of Laura Geringer and Peter Bollinger. • All rights reserved. Published by Scholastic Inc. • Book design by David Saylor.

12 11 10 9 8 7 6 5 4 3 2 1   7 8 9/9 0 1 2/0
Printed in the U.S.A.   08
First Scholastic printing, August 1997

THERE WAS ONCE a beautiful baby girl named Atalanta, born to a father who wanted a son. Now, most parents love their children, but this man, the king of Arcadia, felt no love at all. Cursing the gods for not sending him a boy, he ordered his soldiers to take Atalanta to the top of the tallest mountain and leave her there all alone!

The king's word was law. So the king's men traveled to neighboring Calydon, climbed the highest peak, and left the poor child there. Not knowing she had been left to die, Atalanta looked up at the clouds and she was happy. But as the hours passed, she grew hungry and began to cry.

A mother bear lumbered over to see what could be making so much noise. Gently, she carried the infant back to her cave. And that is how Atalanta, born into a royal family, came to live with the bears.

AS THE YEARS passed, the townspeople told stories about a wild girl sighted from time to time on the cliffs, swinging from vines, somersaulting over streams, and darting swift as an arrow from tree to tree.

Atalanta grew to be a legend in Calydon, where hunters, catching a glimpse of her as she sprang past them, confused her with Artemis, goddess of the hunt. Sometimes they prayed to Atalanta before setting off with their hounds. And those prayers drifted up to Olympus, home of the gods, to Artemis herself, who was not pleased.

One day Artemis, flying across the heavens in her silver moon chariot, looked down, hoping to see this wild girl. Instead, she saw a very handsome boy. About to set off for the hunt, he was kneeling, hands clasped, dark stormy eyes turned up to the sky. Beside him was an enormous dog. Lit by the sunrise, the boy seemed to be looking boldly into his future. And the fire on the horizon, reflected in his eyes, told the goddess of heroic deeds ahead.

Artemis came closer to learn his name from the birds.

"Meleager," they told her, "Prince Meleager. The greatest hunter in Calydon."

There was that name again! Atalanta! Even the birds sang her praises. And fury of furies, what was this? The young hunter was praying — but not to Artemis! No! Instead, Meleager was directing his prayers to that wild girl. To Atalanta!

IN FACT, PRINCE Meleager wasn't praying. He was wishing. Some of his friends had seen Atalanta racing through the woods, and Meleager wanted to see the wild girl, too. He had heard that she spoke only to animals. He had heard that she wrestled like a bear. And he had heard that she was the fastest runner alive.

Lost in thought, Meleager did not notice his father come up behind him. The king put a hand on his son's shoulder. "Your mother and I are worried," he said. "It's time you began to think about finding a wife. But you seem interested only in the hunt — and in your dogs."

Meleager laughed. "My dogs are good company, Father. Especially Alcon." He patted the huge beast by his side. "I promise I'll marry when I find a girl who can hunt as well as Alcon." And, waving farewell, Meleager took off toward the mountain.

Before long, Meleager came upon an enormous bear. Rising to its full height, it towered over the young man. Then, dropping to all fours, it charged.

Meleager drew his dagger and, dodging the animal's big slashing paw, plunged it into the beast's heart. The bear turned and disappeared into the woods.

Meleager and his dog tracked the wounded bear all day. Pausing to rest at a running brook, the hunter dipped his fingers into the water. Suddenly he swung around, rising to his feet. There before him was a tall girl dressed in green, carrying a quiver of arrows on her back and a bow in her hand. When she saw him, she let out a fierce cry, crouched down, and aimed an arrow straight at his heart!

Meleager sprang aside as her arrow whizzed through the air. Flinging her weapons down, Atalanta let out a low growl and jumped him. Then wrapping her arms around him, she squeezed with all her might. Meleager felt crushed, as if the bear he had been chasing were hugging him to death.

YOU MUST BE THE *WILD GIRL*!

Summoning all his strength, he fought out of her grasp. Atalanta kicked him and wrestled him to the ground. They battled one another for a long time until, growing weary, they rested side by side in the grass.

Afraid she would run away, Meleager gently put his hand on Atalanta's hair and touched her face. "Don't go," he said softly.

She blinked, startled, but did not flee. Then, lightly, she touched his face, exclaiming in wonder.

Suddenly the stories about Atalanta that Meleager had heard as a boy came back to him. He recalled that she had been abandoned as a baby and raised by bears. Had she attacked him to protect her animal family? It was all so strange. And stranger still was the sudden feeling that filled his heart.

FTER THAT DAY, Meleager never hunted a bear again. The handsome prince and Atalanta hunted together, from morning to night, with Alcon by their side. They spoke a language of gestures and signs, and they understood each other very well.

Word spread across the land that Meleager, heir to the throne, had chosen his future queen — Atalanta, the wild girl who could not speak.

Meleager's mother was not happy with this news. "When you were born," she told Meleager, "the three Fates visited me. One held in her hands a great ball of thread. 'Queen Althea,' she said, 'your child's life will shine as brightly as this golden thread.'

"The second, taller than the first, carried a spindle. 'I will weave that golden thread into dark places so that it shines even brighter,' she said.

"But the third Fate, who held a giant pair of scissors, said: 'I will cut that golden thread, and his life shall end as soon as this wood has burned to ashes!' and she threw a stick into the flames."

The queen took a blackened stick of wood from a box she kept by her bedside and shook it angrily at Meleager. Her son turned pale.

"I pulled that burning stick out of the fire," Queen Althea went on, "and stamped out the flames. I hid it away here in this box, where I could guard it with my life. Nobody knows this secret but me. And now you know it, too."

BUT *WHY* HAVE YOU TOLD ME, MOTHER? I WOULD RATHER NOT HAVE KNOWN.

EVER SINCE THAT TIME, MELEAGER, WHENEVER YOU'RE IN DANGER, I'M VISITED BY DREAMS OF FIRE. I HAVE THEM *NOW*, MY SON. I FEEL THAT WILD GIRL WILL LEAD YOU TO *DESTRUCTION!*

ATALANTA? YOU ARE WRONG, MOTHER. I LOVE HER WITH ALL MY HEART. IF I GO UP IN FLAMES FOR THAT LOVE, THEN I ACCEPT MY FATE.

OST OF THE gods had a favorite monster. And they used their monsters to punish people who made them angry. But Artemis had no monster. So she went to visit her brother Hades, King of the Dead.

"Imagine for a moment that I were in your power," she said. "And let's say that on earth I led a very evil life. Which of your monsters would you call to punish me? I want your worst."

He smiled. "The Furies, of course," he answered.

"Then let me see your Furies," she demanded.

So he summoned the three terrible hags, with their fiery brass wings and claws and whips. And to these witches of scorching flame and smoke Artemis assigned a task. From the tear-soaked mud of the River Styx in the Land of the Dead, they were to mold her a beast more dangerous than any on earth.

IT'S NO ORDINARY MONSTER I WANT — NO MANY-ARMED, MANY-HEADED THING THAT WILL SCARE OFF MY LITTLE WILD GIRL. OH, NO! AFTER ALL, SHE'S THE GREATEST HUNTER IN THE LAND, IS SHE NOT? COME, LADIES. GIVE ME A BEAST WORTHY OF ATALANTA'S SKILL.

And so the Furies went to work, making a wild boar to do away with the wild girl.

"At last I have my very own monster!" Artemis cried. Then, leaving her moon chariot behind, she leaped onto the boar's back and rode it straight to Calydon.

CHILD OF THE BEAR CLAN, *BEWARE.* I AM *STILL* QUEEN OF THE HUNT.

And at that very moment, Queen Althea, tossing feverishly in her bed, moaned and cried out in her sleep, plagued by yet another dream of her son Meleager with a ring of fire around his head.

HE WILD BOAR ran through the forests and fields of Calydon, spreading terror through the land. It kicked houses apart with its hooves. It trampled great fields of corn, tore through vineyards, uprooted orchards, and attacked herds of grazing cattle. The few people who saw it and escaped told stories of three screaming hags with brass wings riding the monster, one on top of the other like a tower of bats.

Soon shepherds refused to tend their flocks. Farmers were scared to harvest their crops.

"I'll hunt this boar," Meleager said to his father. "I'll bring its head home as my trophy."

"Alone?" asked his father.

"With Atalanta, Father. You've never seen her hunt. She can match Artemis arrow for arrow."

His father shook his head, smiling. At last, his son was in love. He put his hand on Meleager's head and held it there a moment, as if to bless him. "You and Atalanta will hunt the boar," he said, "but not alone."

I N ANSWER TO the king's call, there came to Calydon a hunting party of brave men. Theseus, who had slain the Minotaur, and Jason, soon to be leader of the Argonauts, were among them. For three days, the heroes feasted. On the fourth, they gathered for the hunt.

Meleager appeared with Atalanta by his side. The hunters stared. Many of them had heard of her, but none had expected her to be so beautiful. She looked around solemnly at the company of heroes, and then boldly took her place amongst them.

Sounding his horn, Meleager signaled the hunters to fan out across the valley, surrounding the mouth of a canyon where the boar was known to hide in the brush. The men yelled and beat their shields with their spears.

With a snort of rage, the boar rushed forth, scattering the hunters. Atalanta strung an arrow to her bow and let it fly. Roaring in pain and fury, the brute galloped straight toward Atalanta. The sound of its hooves echoed through the woods like an avalanche of boulders hurtling down a mountain.

Atalanta did not run. She notched another arrow and stood her ground, sending her next shot straight into the wild boar's heart. But Artemis, watching from her moon chariot, would not let her pet die. Forged by the Furies in the Land of the Dead, fueled by the fires of jealousy, it kept on coming, bearing down upon the wild girl.

With a piercing war cry, Meleager flung himself in front of the monster, hurling his spear as he ran. Now the mad boar turned from its path and rushed toward Meleager, who leaped clear over it. Before it could charge him again, he swung his sword in a slashing arc. The beast fell with the force of the blow. Then the others closed in, and this time even the goddess of the moon could not spur the Wild Boar of Calydon to rise.

Now the king came forward. "My son, let's take a moment to thank the gods for sparing us today." And he knelt down, praying to Artemis, goddess of the hunt, never guessing it was she who had sent the boar in the first place!

Meleager laughed. "I'll kneel to *my* goddess, Father," he declared. "She is queen of the hunt and my future queen as well!" And he knelt before Atalanta.

As soon as the words were out of his mouth, the sky blackened, the wind rose, and the forest was filled with the sound of beating wings. Swooping down upon the young man were three giant batlike witches, who surrounded him in a ring of fire. Meleager's hair stood up around his head like a lion's mane, his face lit in the gloom by a halo of flame.

Atalanta screamed and tried to stab the horrible hags with her dagger. But the Furies only cackled and cracked their whips. She opened her mouth, but no sound came.

ATALANTA! ATALANTA!

MELEAGER!

It was the first word she had ever spoken in his language. It echoed in the valley, bouncing off the tall cliffs, tunneling through the caves, reverberating through the trees, flying straight as an arrow into the heart of Queen Althea, awaiting the return of Meleager from the hunt. And at that moment the mother knew she had lost her son forever.

RTEMIS LOOKED DOWN from her moon chariot and was not happy.

It was not the handsome Meleager she had meant to punish, but there he was, the loyal Alcon by his side, feverishly pursued by those ugly Furies.

And there was her rival, Atalanta, still alive. Weeping her way through the forest, she was looking for Meleager. Yet even in her grief, she was running so swiftly and so gracefully that Artemis couldn't turn her eyes away.

It was hard to go on hating Atalanta. After all, Artemis loved the hunt above all else, and the girl was so very good at it. Together, she and Meleager hunted like gods. What a mess Artemis had made of things, all because of her stupid jealousy!

Slowly, Artemis descended in her moon chariot. She found Meleager reeling back and forth through the trees, all three Furies sitting on his back.

Just then, Atalanta burst into the clearing. She ran to Meleager, and he fell into her arms. Tenderly, she cradled his head in her lap. The Furies screeched, not letting him rest.

Artemis remembered Meleager's face when he had first seen the Furies. He had looked like a lion in a ring of fire. And, like a lion, Atalanta had fought fiercely and loyally by his side. The goddess had an idea. She encircled the prince and the wild girl in silvery fog, hiding them from the searching red eyes of the hags from Hades.

"The gods are kind after all," whispered Meleager, smiling up at Atalanta.

And when the fog lifted, two regal lions sat calmly side by side, staring at the Furies with a faraway look in their eyes. Screaming, the hags flapped away. And once again, it was peaceful in the forest of Calydon.

A legend grew in the region. It was said that two golden lions, with fur that glowed like fire, hunted in the company of a huge bear and a giant hound. Some said they were immortal. Some said they were pets of the goddess Artemis, who saw that no harm came to them. And some said they were the spirits of Prince Meleager and Atalanta, the wild girl, who once lived in a bear cave deep in the woods, spoke the language of animals, and could outrun the gods and goddesses of Mount Olympus.

Years later, when Jason, leader of the quest for the Golden Fleece, called upon the heroes of Greece to join him, it was said that Atalanta could not resist the call and, taking her human shape once more, claimed her place among the great warriors for one last adventure. But that, of course, is another story.